DATE			

THE ADVENTURES OF ARCHIE FEATHERSPOON

Cathy Stefanec Ogren

Illustrated by
Jack E. Davis

ALADDIN

New York   London   Toronto   Sydney   Singapore

For Punkin.

First edition March 2002
Text copyright © 2002 by Cathy Stefanec Ogren
Illustrations copyright © 2002 by Jack E. Davis

Aladdin Paperbacks
An imprint of Simon & Schuster
Children's Publishing Division
1230 Avenue of the Americas
New York, NY 10020

Book design by Debra Sfetsios
The text of this book was set in Century ITC Book.

Printed and bound in the United States of America

10 9 8 7 6 5 4 3 2 1

Library of Congress Cataloging-in-Publication Data
Stefanec Ogren, Cathy.
The adventures of Archie Featherspoon / by Cathy Stefanec Ogren.
p. cm.
Summary: A young boy with a knack for creating unusual inventions when he should be helping his mother on the farm finds a use for them when he is made sheriff of a town in Texas and must get rid of a gang of no-good bullies.
ISBN 0-689-84284-8
[1. Inventions—Fiction. 2. Tall tales.] I. Title
PZ7.S8155 Ad 2002   Fic—dc 21   00-052229

THE ADVENTURES OF ARCHIE FEATHERSPOON

Twistin' and Turnin'

"Archie Featherspoon, what in tarnation are you doing in that barn?" called Ma.

Archie stuffed his newest invention into his sturdy knapsack. "It's a surprise," he said.

Ma marched through the door with a bag of seed in her hand. "Are you workin' on another one of those crazy contraptions?"

Archie smiled shyly. "You'll see."

Ma held up the bag of seed. "Corn, Archie, corn. You're supposed to be plantin' corn."

Ma Featherspoon could plow a field better than most men, and coax her hens to lay enough eggs to feed the whole state of Texas. The only thing Ma couldn't do was coax Archie to do his chores.

Archie was different from most boys in the days of the Wild West. He was as tall as a cornstalk on the Fourth of July and just as skinny. He spent most of his days working on some new gadget.

When Archie was supposed to be milking the cows, he was mixing a concoction to keep bears away. When he was supposed to be feeding the chickens, he was making another pair of his snappy stretch overalls. And when he was supposed to be cleaning the horse stalls, he was working on a spring-fed, rock-a-bye bed. His latest invention was high-flying rainbow rockets. Each was a different size and had a special surprise inside for Ma's birthday.

Ma looked at the sky. "Could be a storm brewin'. I'm goin' to town for some feed. Mind you get that corn planted before I get back, and I'll cook you up some of my famous chicken."

Archie smacked his lips. He would do anything for a bite of Ma's hot, crispy chicken. He picked up his knapsack. He shoved the bag of corn seed inside with his bear powder and rockets and headed toward the field.

On his way, a shadow passed over the sun. The wind picked up. It slapped at the dust in the field.

Archie set to work, sticking corn seed in the ground as dust danced around him. Within moments, the wind and the dust joined, and the short-lasting twister of '75 struck. It swallowed Archie

Featherspoon and his high-flying rain-bow rockets. It jumbled and whipped Archie across the plains, spit him out in a pint-sized, lawless town, and vanished.

New Sheriff in Trigger Toe

Archie was in a daze. He stumbled into the local sheriff's office and collapsed into an empty chair.

A crowd of people burst through the door.

"He's here. He's here," shouted a freckle-faced girl. "He's sitting right there in the sheriff's chair."

"Saints be praised!" cried a lady in a canary yellow bonnet.

"He looks kind of puny for a sheriff," said a pudgy little man.

"Well, he ain't no Texas Ranger. That's for dang sure," hooted a wrinkled old cowpoke.

Archie stared at the crowd. "Sheriff?" he said.

"That's right," said a man with a hooked nose. "You're the sheriff we've been waiting for."

"Not me!" exclaimed Archie. "I'm just a kid. I have to get home to plant corn and give Ma her birthday surprise."

"No time," declared the pudgy little man. "You're the new sheriff of Trigger Toe, Texas." He pulled Archie to his feet and pinned a shiny star on Archie's red plaid shirt. "Quick, swear him in. Buster and the three Bully Boys are on their way."

"Who are Buster and the Bully Boys?" Archie asked.

"Trouble," answered the man with the hooked nose.

The wrinkled old cowpoke hooted. "They're more than trouble. They're meaner than a one-eyed grizzly, and they're uglier than a skinned rattle-snake."

Archie Featherspoon gulped. "I'm not old enough to be a sheriff. Ma wouldn't let me."

"She'd be proud of you," said the man with the hooked nose.

"But what about the other sheriff?" asked Archie.

"Gone," answered the pudgy little man. "Buster and the Bully Boys ran him clear out of the state."

Archie felt the earth shake under his feet.

"Look!" cried the freckle-faced girl, staring out the window. "Way out there. A dust storm!"

"Ain't no dust storm," sputtered the wrinkled old cowpoke. "My guess, it's Buster and the Bully Boys."

"It's high time someone taught those hoodlums to obey the law," said the man

with the hooked nose. "And that someone is you, Sheriff."

As Buster and the Bully Boys got
closer, fear froze on the faces of the
townsfolk.

"Gracious heavens," pleaded the lady
in the canary yellow bonnet. "Please
save us."

A Corny Idea

Archie peeked out of the sheriff's office and stared at the swirling ball of dust headed toward them. He gazed back at the frightened townsfolk. "I sure do wish Ma was here. She would know what to do."

"Well, your ma ain't here," said the wrinkled old cowpoke. "So you better think of somethin' mighty quick."

"Hives!" shouted the pudgy little man. "I'm breaking out in hives."

Sure enough, as Archie watched, giant red hives were popping out on the pudgy little man's face faster than corn popping over a hot fire. And just as quickly, an idea popped into Archie's head.

"Do something, Sheriff," cried the freckle-faced girl.

Lickety-split, Archie Featherspoon grabbed the ink pen off the sheriff's desk and began drawing big black dots all over his face.

"Dad gum! What do you think yer doin', Sheriff?" snapped the wrinkled old cowpoke.

"Corn pox!" exclaimed Archie. "I've got the dreaded disease called corn pox!"

"How are black spots going to keep Buster and the Bully Boys out of here?" asked the pudgy little man, scratching his hives.

"Don't you know? Corn pox is very contagious and makes corn grow out of your ears."

"Sounds silly to me," snorted the man with the hooked nose.

"Not if it sends Buster and the Bully Boys packing as soon as they see the sheriff," said the pudgy little man.

"Can Buster and the Bully Boys read?" asked Archie.

The wrinkled old cowpoke hooted. "Nope. They ain't never had no schoolin'. Can't tell pox from socks."

Archie reached in his knapsack for something and then flung his knapsack on his back. He took a poster from the sheriff's office that said: NO BATHING IN THE HORSE TROUGHS and turned to the townsfolk. "I'm going now," he said. "I'm going to face Buster and the Bully Boys. Tell my ma I love her."

"Oh my goodness, my goodness," sniffed the lady in the canary yellow bonnet. "I pray this works."

Archie Featherspoon timidly walked out to the dusty street.

The townsfolk shut themselves up in the jail. "Remember," they said, "we're all behind you."

Bully Boy Battle Begins

When Archie Featherspoon saw the gruesome foursome ride into town, his knees began to shake like the tail of an angry rattler.

Buster and the Bully Boys howled like

a pack of hungry wolves when they saw Archie with a shiny star on his chest.

Buster slid off his horse. He pointed his stubby finger at Archie. It matched the cigar he had clenched between his crooked, yellow teeth. "Get the real sheriff, kid," sneered Buster.

Archie's teeth chattered as he pulled himself up as tall as he could. "I *am* the real sheriff," he squeaked.

"Haw, haw," bellowed Buster. "You're just a baby with black spots all over your face."

"I'm not a baby," said Archie. "I'm the sheriff, and I have corn pox. Now get out of town before you and your friends get corn pox, too."

The three Bully Boys backed away from Archie.

"See that sign?" said Archie, pointing to the poster from the sheriff's office. "It says, DANGER: KEEP AWAY! CORN POX DISEASE."

"Never heard of no corn pox," muttered Buster. "Let me have a look-see."

By this time, Archie was very nervous. "Don't come near," he shouted. "Corn pox is contagious. First come the big black spots and then corn starts growing out of your ears."

Archie reached up to his head and knocked his ear twice with his fist. He dropped two corn seeds into the dusty street.

"Seeds in my ears!" Archie screeched. "Next comes the corn. Save me, Ma!"

The three Bully Boys began shaking in their saddles.

"Let's get out of here," pleaded one Bully Boy.

"I don't want no corncobs growing out of my ears," a second Bully Boy said.

"Maybe this town ain't worth all the trouble," grumbled Buster.

Meanwhile, Archie had become so nervous that he was sweating drops of water from his forehead like a spring rain shower.

Buster took notice. "Hey kid, what's that running off your face?"

Archie swiped the back of his hand across his forehead. It came back black. Archie Featherspoon knew his plan had failed.

Ride the Rocket

"Are you trying to make me a fool?" growled Buster.

"No," squeaked Archie. "I'm just trying to get you out of town."

"Nobody tells me to get out of town," bellowed Buster.

The townsfolk watched in horror as Buster picked up Archie and tossed him into the middle of the street.

Archie rolled like a tumbleweed. The high-flying rainbow rockets spilled out of his knapsack.

The cigar-smoking Buster snatched them. "What are these?"

Archie grabbed them back. "They're a birthday surprise for my ma."

The Bully Boys howled.

"Gimme them, kid," said Buster.

"No," said Archie. "These are for Ma."

Buster picked up Archie. He puffed smoke in his face. Archie's skinny legs dangled in the air as he tightened his grip on the rockets.

"Gimme them!" Buster roared.

"Never!" shouted Archie.

Buster was as mad as a wet hen. He puffed harder on his cigar. Fiery ashes showered the rockets.

The Bully Boys surrounded Archie.

Buster dropped more ashes on the rockets. "If you don't gimme them rockets, me and my boys will . . ."

Hiss! One of the fiery ashes set off a rainbow rocket.

Clinging to his knapsack and the rest of the rockets, Archie Featherspoon shot into the air. He whizzed up, down, and around in circles. It was the ride of his life.

Archie wasn't as strong as most boys, but he was clever. By leaning and pulling on the fiery rocket, Archie was able to dip and swoop around Buster and the Bully Boys.

The outlaws stood bug-eyed, staring at him.

"The kid sheriff is flying!" shouted one Bully Boy.

Archie reached into his knapsack and pulled out his bear powder. He circled the outlaws below and dusted them with the powder.

Buster and the Bully Boys fell into fits of sneezing and coughing.

Using the fiery tail of the flying rocket, Archie lit another rocket from his knapsack. It exploded. Enormous clouds of pink and blue smoke filled the sky.

"It's the end of the world!" shouted the second Bully Boy.

Again and again Archie attacked. He used the straps on his snappy stretch overalls as a slingshot and pelted corn seeds at the Bully Boys.

The gruesome foursome looked like ants running around on a hot griddle.

"Yee-haa!" shouted Archie.

Archie sent another rocket whirling through the air. It found its target in Buster's lumpy behind.

"Yeow!" shrieked Buster as he jumped into the horse trough to cool his aching backside.

"Let's skedaddle before it's too late!" yelled the third Bully Boy.

"Get me out of here," Buster hollered at the three Bully Boys. "I've had enough of this kid and his tricks!"

The gruesome foursome scrambled for their horses. Faster than the flick of a frog's tongue, Buster and the Bully Boys disappeared.

Long Stretch Home

Archie Featherspoon circled the street a few more times before his rocket skidded to a stop.

"Jumpin' Jehoshaphat," whooped the wrinkled old cowpoke. "We got ourselves a real hero."

"Will you stay and be our sheriff?" asked the man with the hooked nose.

Archie shook his head and took off the shiny star. "I can't be your sheriff. If I don't get home, the corn won't get planted. If the corn doesn't get planted, Ma won't make her famous chicken, and I won't be able to surprise her with my high-flying rainbow rockets."

"But your rockets are gone," said the freckle-faced girl.

Archie looked around.

Pieces of rockets littered the ground. All were gone except one, and that had been trampled by Buster's horse.

Archie picked up the crippled rocket and hugged it. A tear caught in his eye.

"No birthday surprise for Ma," he sniffed.

The townsfolk had heavy hearts for Archie's dilemma.

"You're a good boy," said the lady in the canary yellow bonnet. "You saved our town."

The pudgy little man agreed. "Your ma would be right proud of you."

Archie got a determined look in his eye. "Even if my high-flying rainbow rockets are gone, I can still get home and plant the rest of this corn seed for Ma. How far to Boot Junction, Texas?" asked Archie.

"About thirty miles southwest as the crow flies," said the wrinkled old cowpoke.

Archie knew what he had to do. He checked the direction of the wind. He did some figures in his head, picked up the corn seed, and grabbed his last high-flying rainbow rocket. He shimmied up a tree, hooked the straps of his snappy stretch overalls to a sturdy branch, and aimed himself toward home.

"Pull so I can fly to my ma."

The townsfolk grabbed Archie's bony ankles. They pulled, and they pulled, and they pulled.

When Archie was just at the right angle, he yelled, "Let go!"

Archie Featherspoon shot out of his snappy stretch overalls like a bullet out of a rifle.

"Good luck," shouted the townsfolk.

But Archie didn't hear them. He sailed across the plains in his red plaid shirt and underwear. He clutched the corn seed and his last rainbow rocket.

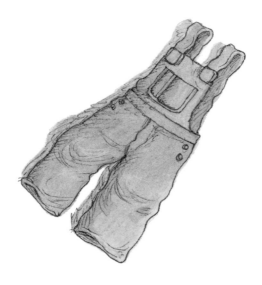

Pink Umbrellas and Crispy Chicken

Archie's figures were a bit off. Instead of landing in the cornfield, he crashed into the chicken coop.

There was a ruckus. Feet and feathers flew.

Archie was picking straw out of his hair when he heard Ma. "Come out, varmint!" she yelled.

Dragging his rainbow rocket, Archie stepped out of the chicken coop.

"Archie Featherspoon, what in tarnation are you doin' in there in your red underwear?"

"Well, Ma . . ." began Archie.

"And why isn't that cornfield planted?"

"Well, Ma . . ." Archie began again.

Ma stamped her foot. "Archie Featherspoon, what am I goin' to do with you? All day long you fiddle with those crazy contraptions of yours. There's work to be done around here."

"But Ma . . ." said Archie.

"And don't think I'll be cookin' my

famous chicken for you tonight, either."

Ma's eyes sparked. She was so mad she was spitting fire.

Archie's last high-flying rainbow rocket began to sizzle.

"Ma, watch out!" he shouted.

Archie grabbed the bag of corn seed and hopped on the rocket just as it took off. He steered clear of Ma and headed toward the cornfield.

Much to Ma's amazement, Archie guided the rocket up and down the rows, planting corn faster than a barn owl goes for a plump mouse. Just as Archie dropped the last seed into the dirt, the rocket exploded.

Archie crashed to the ground. Smoke and pink umbrellas filled the air.

"Archie! My baby!" shrieked Ma. She ran and gathered him into her arms. "Are you hurt? Say something."

Archie's belly let out a growl louder than a hungry bear.

At that moment, one last pink umbrella with "Happy Birthday, Ma!" written on it floated through the air and landed in Ma's lap.

"Why, Archie Featherspoon," she said. "You are full of surprises. I reckon someday you might even be president."

"Aw, Ma." Archie smiled up at Ma and rubbed his empty belly. "I sure could go for some of your hot, crispy chicken."

"I do declare," said Ma. "Any boy who's as clever as you are deserves to be fed a whole flock of chickens."

That night Archie Featherspoon was fuller than a running creek after a summer storm. Before he tumbled into his spring-fed, rock-a-bye bed, he gave Ma a birthday hug as big as the whole state of Texas.